5/2013

This book belongs to

_____

Isabella
STAR OF THE STORY

story by Jennifer Fosberry • pictures by Mike Litwin

sourcebooks
jabberwocky

For Joan, who always was one, and Dana, who studied to be one, and Toots, who never got a degree but started a place anyway, and for Kiersten, who continues the family tradition. And for all the other librarians that I am not related to by blood, but only by books. Thanks for everything.

- JF

For Stan & Jan, Mercer, Maurice, Shel, C. S., John, Judy, Donald, Dr. Seuss, and especially to Mom—all of whom fostered my love of reading at an early age.

- ML

Published by Sourcebooks Jabberwocky, an imprint of Sourcebooks, Inc.
P.O. Box 4410, Naperville, Illinois 60567-4410
(630) 961-3900
Fax: (630) 961-2168
www.jabberwockykids.com

Library of Congress Cataloging-in-Publication data is on file with the publisher.

Source of Production: Oceanic Graphic Printing, Kowloon, Hong Kong, China
Date of Production: January 2013
Run Number: 19207

Printed and bound in China.
OGP 10 9 8 7 6 5 4 3 2 1

"Slow down Isabella," the father said, "those books aren't going anywhere."

"Oh yes they are—some lucky books are going home with me!" the little girl said.

"And my name is NOT Isabella."

JOAN GILLIGAN
MEMORIAL
LIBRARY

"Then whose library card is this?" asked the mother.

"I am **Peter Pan**, and I am flying two stars to the right and straight on to the children's room."

"Well, Peter," the mother said, "I know that you will never **OUTGROW** a good story."

"Mrs. DARLING, let's start with this one," the little girl said.

"And my name is NOT Peter."

"Then who just
handed me this book?"
asked the mother.

"I am Goldilocks, and I am searching for a book that is not too short and not too long."

"Well, Goldie," the father said, "then we should look for some *fairy tales*."

"ENCHANTING idea and even a little bit GRIM," the little girl said.

"And my name is NOT Goldilocks."

"Then who will tell me
if this book is just right?"
asked the father.

"I am **Captain Nemo**, and
I am on a legendary dive."

"Aye, Aye Captain,"
the father said,
"20,000 leagues we go!"

"I just hope it's
not TOO DEEP,"
the little girl said.

*"And my name is
NOT Captain Nemo."*

"Then just who is in
charge of this search?"
asked the father.

"I am *Black Beauty,* and I am galloping off to greener pastures for a fantastic tale."

"Well, *Giddyup My Beauty*," said the mother. "Do you want to take this one out?"

"NEIGHHH...
I mean—yes, please!"
the little girl said.

*"And my name is
NOT Black Beauty."*

"Then who will trot over here and put that book in the bag?" asked the mother.

"I am Alice, and I am following a little white rabbit on an epic adventure."

"Alice, don't lose your head," the mother said. "Are you sure you want this book?"

"We would be MAD not to take that book home with us," the little girl said.

"And my name is NOT Alice."

"Then who is going to use their library card today?" asked the mother.

"I am DOROTHY, and I have been twisted away to a wonderful world but now I am trying to get back."

"Well, Dorothy," the librarian said, "Just FOLLOW THE YELLOW BRICK ROAD to the checkout desk, dear."

"Yes, I think we have enough books and there really is NO PLACE LIKE HOME," the little girl said.

"And my name is NOT Dorothy."

"Then whose name IS
on the library card?"
asked the librarian.

"It's me, *Isabella*," said the little girl.
"Just someone who loves a good book."

And as the little girl and her family headed
home, the father said, "Isabella, it's awfully late.
There will only be time for one story before bed."

"That's okay," Isabella said. "We'll pick one for tonight
and we can curl up and read the rest of them

...tomorrow."

stories for all time...

PETER PAN BY J. M. BARRIE

The story of Peter Pan is a story about a boy who wouldn't grow up. It was written by J. M. Barrie, or Jamie, in 1904 and he was a man who loved to play. Jamie was born on May 9, 1860 in a group of row houses called the Tenements in Kirriemuir, Scotland. He was the seventh child and often spoke about how poor his family was; however, this was not entirely true as his father had good work as a hand loom weaver. Jamie's mother read and told stories to the family and Jamie would create plays for the neighbors.

When Jamie grew up he moved to London and lived near Kensington Gardens. He walked Porthos, his great Saint Bernard, there every day. In the garden he met the Llewelyn Davies family, which had five young boys. He played pirates and Indians and told stories to them and became a close family friend. He even became the boys' guardian after their parents both died of cancer. He was said to have written *Peter Pan* based on these boys. It was written first as a play called *Peter and Wendy* and was staged in London. After secret rehearsals, the play opened and was a huge success. Jamie died in 1937, but he gifted the copyright to the Great Ormond Hospital for Sick Children in London which received all royalty money until 2007 (when copyright ran out).

DID YOU KNOW: In professional plays, the character of Peter Pan has always been played by a woman, as originally suggested by Jamie's agent from the first performance. At the first production of the play in New York City, actress Maude Adams asked the audience to clap if they believed in fairies.

GOLDILOCKS AND THE THREE BEARS

The story of the poor bears who have their breakfast sampled, chairs broken, and beds slept in by an uninvited guest started as a folk tale in England. Robert Southey (1774-1843) was a poet and wrote down the story, originally titled "The Story of the Three Bears," into his book *The Doctor* which was published in 1837. When Joseph Jacobs reprinted it in *English Fairy Tales,* he also found an earlier tale called "Scrapefoot" which had a fox visiting the bears. In the original Southey telling, the intruder is a nasty, bad old lady. Over time and various retellings, it turned out that children preferred a pretty young girl. She started out with silver hair and eventually became the golden-haired child that is in most versions today. Also, the bears started as three different sizes and it wasn't until an 1878 version that they were identified as Papa Bear, Mama Bear, and Baby Bear.

DID YOU KNOW: There are now several different endings for the story.

20,000 LEAGUES UNDER THE SEA BY JULES VERNE

Jules Verne was always interested in travel. He was born in France in 1828 and for a while his family lived on an island in the Loire River before moving to Nantes. It was a port city with boats that sailed to the ocean, and he visited the docks regularly. Once he paid to take the place of a young cabin boy on the *Coralie,* a ship that set sail for the West Indies. This worked until his father found out about his scheme later that morning and came by steamboat to take him home. When Jules was nine years old, he and his brother were sent to boarding school. This is where he further developed his interest in travel, exploration, and scientific advances. These concepts show in his later adventure stories, including *Twenty Thousand Leagues under the Sea, Around the World in Eighty Days,* and *Journey to the Center of the Earth.* Many of his stories use creations of his imagination that were not invented until much later. These include submarines, helicopters, diving suits, and plastics. The adventures he wrote involve journeys through air, space, and underwater before any method of such transportation was invented. Because of his method of adding scientific explanations to his stories, he is often referred to as the father of science fiction.

DID YOU KNOW: An unpublished work of Jules Verne, *Paris in the Twentieth Century,* was found in a safe that had been passed down to his great-grandson. It was published and became a bestseller in Paris 90 years after Jules' death. It predicted cars, gas stations, computers, and giant bookstores.

BLACK BEAUTY BY ANNA SEWELL

Anna Sewell was born in England in 1820. She and her family were Quakers and had compassion for those less fortunate, including animals. Anna's mother was a bestselling author of the time, writing books for children, which Anna helped to edit. Anna injured herself as a child and was not able to walk without assistance, a condition that worsened as she grew older. She was fearless and did not let this stop her from doing good works. She was able to get around by driving a horse carriage. She witnessed the way that horses were treated as they worked in Victorian England. When she became housebound, she decided to write a book about their poor conditions. She hoped to encourage "kindness and better treatment of horses." Much of the story was transcribed by her mother. Anna narrated the story from the horse's point of view, as if it were a recollection of his life told in his own words. This was an unusual way to tell the story at that time. Anna sold *Black Beauty: His Grooms and Companions: The Autobiography of a Horse* for only 20 pounds, and it was first published in 1877. She died a few months later and never saw the full popularity of her book or the changes made to the way that horses were treated largely attributed to her story.

DID YOU KNOW: *Black Beauty* is one of the bestselling books of all time, with an estimate of over 50 million copies sold.

ALICE'S ADVENTURES IN WONDERLAND BY LEWIS CARROLL

The Reverend Charles Lutwidge Dodgson had ten brothers and sisters and made up plays and magazines for them. He was born in 1832 in Daresbury, Chesire where his father was the vicar. That means he was in charge of the church in that community. Charles was also very smart in mathematics, but did not like going away to a boarding school. He was a good student and when he graduated from university, he was appointed as a lecturer in mathematics at Christ Church. This meant he also had to study to be a clergyman and never marry. In his free time he loved to make up stories and was very fond of the nonsense of language and logic. He wrote stories using the Latinized version of his name, Lewis Carroll. This is called a pen name. He was very quiet and proper and sometimes uncomfortable around adults, but he was a good friend and story teller to many of the children of his friends and fellow teachers. One young friend in particular, Alice Liddell, is thought to have inspired his story *Alice's Adventures in Wonderland*, which was published in 1865 and became an immediate success. *Alice through the Looking Glass* was published six years later.

DID YOU KNOW: The original manuscript included drawings done by Lewis Carroll and is in the Widener Library at Harvard University. Charles Lutwidge Dodgson had trouble hearing and spoke with a stutter. Many think this is why he was more comfortable with children than adults.

THE WONDERFUL WIZARD OF OZ BY L. FRANK BAUM

L. Frank Baum was born in 1856 in Chittenango, New York to a very well-off family. He had tutors from England and was a small, frail boy who loved to read. At twelve, his family sent him to military school, but he quickly returned home because he hated it. His father bought Frank his own printing press, and he started a family newspaper. When he grew up, he also went into the newspaper business as an editor (in Averdeen, South Dakota and Chicago), but not before trying many different careers such as theater, chicken breeding, and working as a traveling salesman and storekeeper. Many of his endeavors were ruined when one of his workers stole his money. He always rejected offers from his wealthy mother, as he was determined to take care of his own family. His wife Maud Gage (who was the daughter of a famous women's rights activist) did what she could to keep things together for them and their four boys. Frank was a playful man who loved time spent with the children, and he told stories every night to his sons and eventually to ten or more neighborhood children as well. At the suggestion of his mother-in-law, he began to write out these stories. Originally titled *The Wonderful Wizard of Oz*, the book was published in 1900 and became a bestseller. In 1939 it was made into a movie with Judy Garland as Dorothy, which has become a classic.

DID YOU KNOW: The L in his name stands for Lyman, but nobody ever called him that. When *The Wonderful Wizard of Oz* was made into a movie, the Technicolor portion wanted the shoes to be more colorful, so they became ruby slippers. In the original book, they are actually silver. In Isabella's story, can you find what color we chose for Dorothy's shoes? (Hint: they're on more than one page!)

acknowledgments

I would like to thank the authors of all the books I ever read, for entertaining and educating and inspiring me. I would like to thank all the librarians along the way who put those books in my hands. I would like to thank Chris Spitzel, for helping me find the answers, my parents who kept lots of stacks around the house, and my husband and children for making me work to make you into readers. I would like to thank the good folks at Sourcebooks: Steve Geck for the story spark and editing with as little pain as possible, Helen Nam for being as thrilled with the visual as I am, Dominique Raccah, always, for the vision, Todd Stocke and Kelly Barrales-Saylor for helping to guide this baby through to production, Jillian Bergsma for making me sound smarter than I am, and Aubrey, Kim, Derry, Heather, Sarah, Heidi, Sean, Chris, Valerie, Katie, and everyone else who goes out and shares the Isabella love with the world. And of course thank you to Mike for listening, internalizing, and then using his God-given amazing talent to make things more fantastical than I ever dream of. —**JF**

list of works consulted

BOOKS:

1000 Makers of the Millennium. DK Publishing, Inc. New York, 1999.

Krull, Kathleen, ill. by Kevin Hawkes. *The Road to Oz: Twists, Turns, Bumps, and Triumphs in the Life of L. Frank Baum.* Alfred A. Knopf, New York, 2008.

Perkins, Christine N. *100 Authors Who Shaped World History.* A Bluewood Book, San Mateo, California, 1996.

Schoell, William. *Remarkable Journeys: The Story of Jules Verne.* Morgan Reynolds Publishing, Inc. Greensboro, North Carolina, 2002.

Spirin, Gennady, as retold and illustrator. *Goldilocks and the Three Bears.* Marshall Cavendish Children, Tarrytown, New York, 2009.

Yolen, Jane, ill. Steve Adams. *The Lost Boy. The story of the man who created Peter Pan.* Dutton Children's Books, New York, 2010.

WEBSITES:

"Anna Sewell." Major Authors and Illustrators for Children and Young Adults. Gale, 2002. Gale Biography In Context. Web. 14 Sep. 2012.

Barrie, J. M. "To the Five: A Dedication to 'Peter Pan'." DISCovering Authors. Detroit: Gale, 2003. Gale Student Resources In Context. Web. 14 Sep. 2012.

"Baum, L. Frank (1856-1919)." Encyclopedia of World Biography. Detroit: Gale, 1998. Gale Biography In Context. Web. 14 Sep. 2012.

Greene, Carol. Lewis Carroll, author of Alice in Wonderland. Childrens Press, Chicago, 1992.

Holmes, Roger W. "The Philosopher's `Alice in Wonderland'." DISCovering Authors. Detroit: Gale, 2003. Gale Student Resources In Context. Web. 14 Sep. 2012.

"Lewis Carroll." Encyclopedia of World Biography. Detroit: Gale, 1998. Gale Biography In Context. Web. 14 Sep. 2012.

"L(yman) Frank Baum." Major Authors and Illustrators for Children and Young Adults. Gale, 2002. Gale Biography In Context. Web. 14 Sep. 2012.

"When I was young I longed to write a great novel that should win me fame. Now that I am getting old my first book is written to amuse children. For, aside from my evident inability to do anything 'great,' I have learned to regard fame as a will-o-the-wisp which, when caught, is not worth the possession; but to please a child is a sweet and lovely thing that warms one's heart and brings its own reward."

—L. Frank Baum